LEGO NINJAGO
Masters of Spinjitzu

PIRATES VS. NINJA

ADAPTED BY TRACEY WEST

SCHOLASTIC INC.

ISBN 978-0-545-63643-8

LEGO, the LEGO logo, the Brick and Knob configurations and the Minifigure are trademarks of the LEGO Group. © 2013 The LEGO Group. Produced by Scholastic Inc. under license from the LEGO Group. Published by Scholastic Inc. SCHOLASTIC and associated logos are trademarks and/or registered trademarks of Scholastic Inc.

12 11 10 9 8 7 6 5 4 3 2 1   13 14 15 16 17 18/0
Printed in the U.S.A.   40
This edition first printing, September 2013

PATIENCE, LLOYD!

"*Hii-yah!* Fists of Fury!" Lloyd yelled, pounding his fist into Kai's palm.

Ninja Cole, Jay, Kai, and Zane were training Lloyd in their Ninjago City apartment. It had been their home since evil Lord Garmadon had stolen the *Destiny's Bounty*, their flying ship. But a kitchen was no place to train a ninja. Kai had to use oven mitts for gloves.

"Lloyd, you are late for your next lesson with Nya," said Sensei Wu.

"*Aw!* But when will I learn Spinjitzu?" Lloyd whined.

"Patience," Sensei Wu told him. "Your Spinjitzu will only be unlocked when the key is ready to be found."

Sighing, Lloyd went off to see Kai's sister, Nya, a samurai warrior.

Lloyd found Nya stroking the nose of a four-headed dragon. The great beast was sick.

"One day, he'll be yours," Nya said. "Ultra Dragon is meant for the Green Ninja to ride."

The dragon's four heads roared.

"Looks like he's feeling better," Lloyd said as the dragon flew off.

Lloyd was destined to become the legendary Green Ninja. Sensei Wu sent the ninja to find a better place to train him.

"These will transport you any place you want to go," Sensei said with a smile. "They are bus tokens!"

THE MEGA WEAPON'S POWER

Meanwhile, Lord Garmadon and his crew of Serpentine warriors flew high above Ninjago City aboard the *Destiny's Bounty*, the ancient pirate ship Garmadon had stolen from the ninja. He also had their magical Weapons. Combined, they formed the Mega Weapon.

Lord Garmadon only had one problem. He didn't know how the Weapon worked!

"We spotted something!" one of the crew members cried. He pointed to Ultra Dragon as it flew past the ship.

"Don't let him get away, you slithering idiots!" Garmadon yelled. He pointed the Weapon at the dragon. "Destroy!"

But the Weapon didn't do anything.

Garmadon stormed belowdecks. He pounded the Weapon on a table.

A secret door opened, and an old journal popped out. Lord Garmadon read the story of Captain Soto. The pirate and his crew had sailed the ship two hundred years before.

"This crew sounds like they knew how to handle a ship," Garmadon said. "I wish they were here to show these scaly idiots how it's done!"

Suddenly, the Mega Weapon began to sizzle and smoke.

"What is happening?" Lord Garmadon wailed. "It won't let me let go!"

Then he heard a voice overhead. "All hands on deck! I am Captain Soto!"

PIRATES ON BOARD

Lord Garmadon rushed to the deck. Captain Soto and his pirate crew had come to life! They waved their swords at the snakes.

"I asked for a better crew, and I got it," Lord Garmadon realized. "The Mega Weapon has the power to create!" But using it had left him very weak.

Captain Soto marched up to Lord Garmadon. "I be Captain Soto, Stealer of the Seas!" the pirate snarled. "We are taking back our ship."

Then he turned to his crew. "Lock him and all his reptilian friends in the brig!"

Lord Garmadon was too weak to fight back. The pirates locked him and the Serpentine warriors in the ship's jail.

On deck, Captain Soto discovered that his ship could fly.

"This is too good!" He chuckled as they flew toward Ninjago City. "Just wait till they get a load of us!"

FOLLOW THAT SHIP!

Back in the city, the ninja had found a new place to train: Grand Sensei Dareth's Mojo Dojo. But Dareth was no Sensei Wu.

"I am a karate machine," Dareth bragged. But when he tried to show off his skills, he just got tangled up.

The ninja got busy training Lloyd. Cole showed Lloyd how to break a stack of boards.

Bam! Lloyd broke the boards — and the floor, too!

"With this power, you must be careful," Sensei Wu warned. "You must control it before it controls you."

Then the ninja heard screams outside. The pirates were attacking the city!

"You must stay here," Zane told Lloyd. "Your powers are not ready yet."

A bus pulled up, and the ninja hopped on.

"Follow that ship!" Kai told the driver.

DARETH WALKS THE PLANK

Grand Sensei Dareth wanted to impress the ninja. He jumped onto the pirate ship from a rooftop.

"Surrender, or face the brown ninja!" he cried.

"Pajama Man! Get him!" yelled Captain Soto.

Dareth's silly karate moves were no match for the pirates. They grabbed him and tied him up.

"Keep an eye out for any other masked Pajama People," Captain Soto told his crew.

Back in Ninjago City, Cole, Jay, Kai, and Zane knew that they needed disguises. They put on pirate costumes and sneaked onboard the floating ship.

Captain Soto was making Dareth walk the plank!

The ninja couldn't save Dareth. Captain Soto pushed him off the plank!

"*Aaaaah!*" Dareth screamed as he fell.

"*Yee-hah!*" Lloyd appeared, riding the Ultra Dragon! He swooped down from the sky. The dragon caught Dareth in one of its mouths.

WHO WILL WIN?

"Ninjago!" the four ninja yelled. They used Spinjitzu to transform into their ninja outfits.

Captain Soto looked confused. "More Pajama Men?"

"Ninja versus pirates," Kai said. "Who will win?"

Cole jumped across the deck. He used his scythe to slice the feather off Captain Soto's hat.

The battle had begun!

Three pirates surrounded Kai. He thrust his sword into the deck.

Whap! Whap! Whap! He grabbed the hilt and swung around, kicking the pirates away.

Another pirate charged at Zane. He held a sharp dagger in each hand.

Crack! Zane used his whip to send the pirate flying backward.

Kai and Cole fought off two pirates. Jay had an idea. He used his nunchuks to break open a gumball machine.

The gumballs spilled out onto the deck. *Splat!* The pirates tripped and fell down — and so did Kai and Cole.

"Oops!" Jay said.

A BARREL OF TROUBLE

"Ninjago!" Lloyd yelled. He jumped off the Ultra Dragon and landed on the pirate ship.

Captain Soto charged at Lloyd. Kai jumped between them.

"Lloyd! You're not supposed to be here!" Kai yelled. He stuffed Lloyd in a wooden barrel to keep him safe.

With the barrel over his head, Lloyd couldn't see where he was going. He accidentally bumped into the lever that dropped the ship's anchor.

Then he bumped into Kai. Kai jumped on top of the barrel, and they rolled across the deck together.

Kai fell off the barrel . . . and fell off the ship!

"Whoa!" he screamed.

He grabbed on to the anchor dangling from the ship. He clung to it as the anchor tore up the streets of Ninjago City.

A SURPRISE RESCUE

Back on the *Destiny's Bounty*, Captain Soto attacked Lloyd's barrel.

"Ninjago!" Lloyd cried.

He began to spin, turning into a green tornado of energy. The barrel exploded into pieces.

"I just did Spinjitzu for the first time!" Lloyd cheered.

Down below, Kai and the anchor were about to slam into a gas truck. If they hit it, the explosion would rock Ninjago City.

Up on the ship . . . *bam!* Captain Soto hit Lloyd from behind.

Lloyd fell into the lever that worked the anchor. It pulled the anchor back up to the ship — just in time!

Lloyd powered up with Spinjitzu — but he couldn't control his new abilities. Sizzling green light knocked down the mast of the ship. It crashed onto the ninja, trapping them all.

"You lose, Pajama People," Captain Soto said with an evil grin. "Now you're walking the plank."

Boom! Boom! Boom! The ship began to shake. The pirates looked up, and saw a giant robot stomping toward them.

It was Nya, piloting her giant samurai robot! She picked up the big mast and knocked down the pirate crew. Then she jumped out, slid down the ship's sails, and landed on Captain Soto.

"Who wins between pirates and ninja?" Jay asked. "It's samurai!"

The Ninjago City police rounded up the pirates. "That your ship?" an officer asked the ninja.

Lord Garmadon was flying away on the *Destiny's Bounty*. "You snooze, you lose!"

"Great," Jay sighed. "Lord Garmadon's back, and now he's got our ship?"

Cole mussed Lloyd's hair. "Well, at least we've got this little guy!"

Lloyd grinned. He couldn't wait until he could be the Green Ninja all the time!

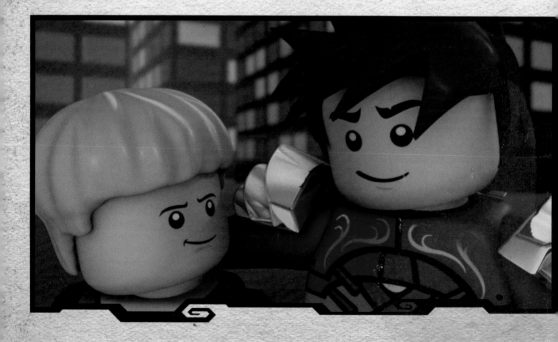

SCHOLASTIC INC.

ADAPTED BY TRACEY WEST

THE GREEN NINJA

NINJAGO Masters of Spinjitzu

LEGO

ISBN 978-0-545-63643-8

12 11 10 9 8 7 6 5 4 3 2 1   13 14 15 16 17 18/0

Printed in the U.S.A.   40

This edition first printing, September 2013

KID STUFF

"We've been training all day," Lloyd complained to his four ninja friends, Cole, Jay, Kai, and Zane.

"We have to get you ready to face your father," Cole reminded him. Lloyd was the Green Ninja — the only one who could take down the evil Lord Garmadon.

"But the latest edition of *Starfarer* just came in to Doomsday Comics," Lloyd said.

"Sorry, Lloyd," Kai said, "but as the Green Ninja, you don't have time for kid stuff."

Nya ran onto the deck of *Destiny's Bounty*, the ninja's flying ship. "Guys! Lord Garmadon has broken into the Ninjago Museum of Natural History."

"Let me guess," Lloyd said. "This mission is too dangerous for me, right?"

"Right!" the four ninja agreed.

Inside the museum, Lord Garmadon held the Mega Weapon. It was a magical Weapon with the power to create.

"Behold . . . the Grundle!" Lord Garmadon cried. He pointed to a skeleton of a huge, fierce-looking beast. "It is now extinct. But when it roamed Ninjago, it could track any ninja."

RISE OF THE GRUNDLE

Lord Garmadon pointed the Mega Weapon at the Grundle skeleton.

"Rise, Grundle!" he commanded.

The Weapon sizzled with blue sparks. Purple energy waves flowed over the skeleton.

The four ninja burst into the museum. Garmadon's Serpentine warriors tried to stop them.

But the ninja were fast. They jumped on top of the Grundle. The snake warriors charged them. They knocked Cole, Jay, and Zane off the Grundle's back.

Kai threw his sword at Lord Garmadon, knocking the Mega Weapon from his hand. The purple energy faded.

"Not again!" Lord Garmadon wailed.

"*Ha-ha!* We stopped him! It didn't work!" Jay cheered.

Lord Garmadon ran off. His snake warriors followed him, carrying a golden sarcophagus along with them.

"They're stealing it!" Kai cried. "After them!"

The ninja raced out of the museum and onto the street. The sarcophagus was heavy, so the snakes dropped it and escaped.

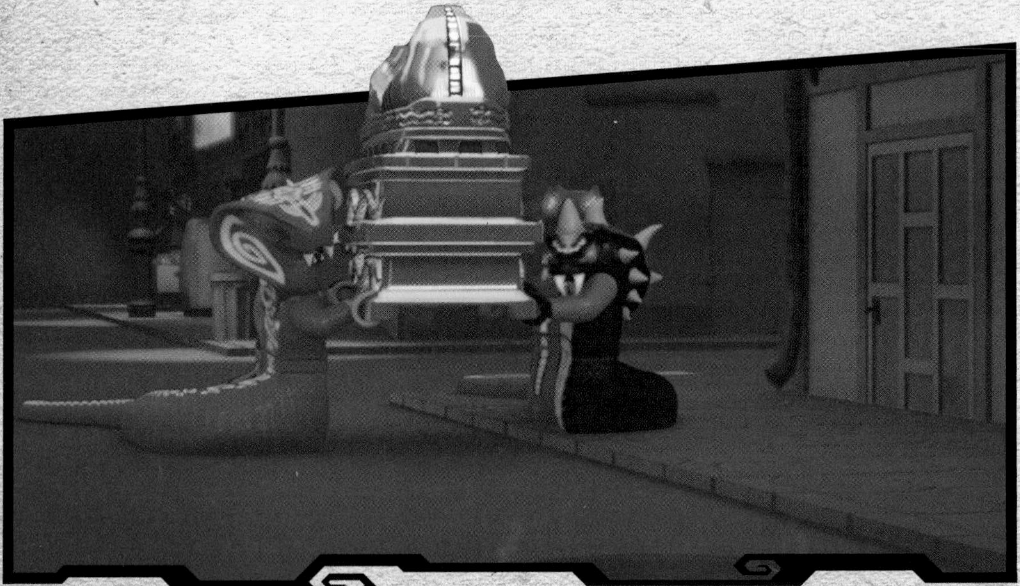

THE INCREDIBLE SHRINKING NINJA

"I don't remember that sarcophagus being so big," Kai remarked.

"Did it grow?" Jay asked.

"Or did we shrink?" wondered Zane.

Suddenly, Kai noticed their reflection in a store window. "Uh, guys?"

"We *shruuuunk*!" Jay screamed.

It was worse than that. The ninja had been turned back into kids!

"I hate being a kid!" Cole wailed. "You can't drive. Nobody listens to you. Oh, no . . . bedtimes!"

"Garmadon must have made us younger with the Mega Weapon," Zane guessed.

At that moment, a police car screeched to a stop next to them.

"Looks like we caught the museum thieves!" the police officer said.

The ninja tried to explain what had really happened, but the police didn't believe them. Cole, Jay, Kai, and Zane spent the night in the police station.

Back at the ship, Nya and Sensei Wu were worried about them.

"Lloyd, you're in charge of the *Bounty* while Nya and I have a look around town," Sensei Wu told him.

ONE ANCIENT MONSTER

The next morning, the police brought the ninja and the sarcophagus back to the museum.

"Thank you," said the director. "But what about the Grundle?" He pointed to an empty display case.

"You don't think it just walked out of here?" Jay wondered.

"It is possible that Garmadon made the Grundle younger, too," Zane said, "and brought it back to life!"

Jay ran up to the grownups. "You guys have to believe us! The Grundle has been brought back to life, and it's on the loose!"

The director and the police just laughed.

"You boys wait here until we call your parents to pick you up," an officer told them.

"We gotta get out of here — like, now!" Cole warned the other ninja.

The ninja pretended to be part of a school group. They sneaked out of the museum.

"This is so humiliating!" Jay wailed.

"We can't use Spinjitzu in these bodies," Zane pointed out. "We are no match for the Grundle."

"Then we have to get back to the *Bounty*!" Kai told his friends.

THE GRUNDLE RETURNS

Rawr! As the ninja hurried away, a loud roar came from the museum. A huge, red beast with sharp claws and teeth jumped off the roof.

It was the Grundle! The great beast hated the sunlight. It stomped off to find a place to sleep until the sun went down. The people of Ninjago screamed and ran when they saw it.

The ninja didn't see the Grundle. They found a pay phone and called the *Destiny's Bounty*.

Lloyd answered the phone. "Where are you?" he asked. "Sensei is out looking for you."

"We can't explain now," Jay said. "Just meet us at Buddy's Pizza in ten minutes — and bring our weapons."

Ten minutes later, Lloyd strolled into the pizza parlor.

"*Pssst!* Lloyd!" Kai whispered.

"Beat it, brat! I'm on a mission," Lloyd said. He thought Kai was just some kid.

"It's me, Kai!" Kai told him.

Lloyd gasped. "Whoa! What happened? You're . . . small!"

Cole, Jay, Kai, and Zane explained how Lord
Garmadon had brought the Grundle to life —
and turned them into kids at the same time.

"We can't defeat the Grundle until we're back
to full strength," Kai said. "We need to find
someone who knows how to fight that thing."

Lloyd grinned. "I think I know just the guy!"

COMIC-BOOK HEROES

Lloyd brought the ninja to a comics shop.

"We're not gonna pick up your stupid comic, Lloyd," Kai complained. "This is serious business!"

Suddenly, Jay let out a happy cry. "Look! A new issue of Daffy Dale!"

"Boys, this is Rufus McAllister, also known as Mother Doomsday," Lloyd said. "He owns this place."

"Rufus, what do you know about the Grundle?" Lloyd asked.

"I know all about that extinct beast," Rufus said. "One, its thick hide can't be hurt by any weapons. Two, it only hunts at night. And three, the only way to defeat it is with light."

The ninja nervously looked out the window. The sun was going down fast.

"The Illuma Sword is the best weapon for fighting a Grundle," Rufus said. "That is, if you can get close enough to use it."

"We'll take the light swords," Kai said eagerly.

"Not so fast," said Rufus. "You'll have to win these swords in a *Starfarer* trivia battle."

"Sign me up!" Lloyd said.

Before the contest started, Lloyd got a message to Sensei Wu.

"There is only one person who can turn the ninja back to normal," Sensei Wu told Nya. They hurried to Mystake's tea shop and explained their problem.

"You need Tomorrow's Tea," the old woman told them. "I should have one here somewhere."

Back at the comic shop, the contest began. Lloyd and two other kids answered questions about the *Starfarer* comic book and its hero, Fritz Donegan. It came down to Lloyd and just one other player.

"Lloyd! Lloyd! Lloyd!" the ninja cheered.

"Here's your final question," Rufus said. "In the latest issue, how does Fritz Donegan escape the Imperial Sludge?"

"B-b-but I didn't read the latest issue," Lloyd stammered.

Just then, the lights in the comic shop flickered. The whole room began to shake.

"It's here," Kai whispered.

ATTACK OF THE GRUNDLE

"What's here?" Rufus asked nervously.

They all looked up at the glass roof. A huge, scary figure loomed above them.

Crunch! A huge, scaly foot stomped down, smashing the glass.

Everyone screamed and ran.

Crash! The Grundle fell through the ceiling. The ninja quickly ran and pulled on ninja outfits on display in the store. They each grabbed an Illuma Sword and charged the Grundle.

Hii-yaah! One by one, they attacked the Grundle, but the monster swatted them away like flies.

The Grundle hovered over them, its huge jaw open. Green slime dripped from its mouth.

"*Aaaaah!*" the ninja screamed.

"I'll take care of this," Lloyd said. He created a ball of energy in his hands and hurled it at the Grundle.

Swat! The Grundle knocked down Lloyd with its tail.

Suddenly, Nya and Sensei Wu burst through the door.

Sensei Wu held up a jar of glowing liquid. "Use this! It will turn time forward. You will grow up and the Grundle will turn back into a pile of bones."

He tossed the jar to Jay.

"Wait!" Cole cried. "What will happen to Lloyd? He'll grow old, too."

"Just do it!" Lloyd cried.

"We can't take away your childhood," Jay said. "It's not fair."

The Grundle charged at the ninja, and they fell backward. The jar flew out of Jay's hands and landed in Lloyd's lap.

Lloyd stood up. He threw the jar at the Grundle. It hit him in the nose, and a purple mist floated out.

THE GREEN NINJA

   Purple light swirled, and the Grundle whirled around as the magic tea took effect. Then the great beast quickly crumbled into a pile of bones.

   When the dust cleared, Kai, Jay, Cole, and Zane stood up. They were taller — and older.

   "We're not kids anymore," Cole realized.

Lloyd slowly got to his feet. He was taller. His hair was thicker. His voice was deeper.

"I'm . . . older," he said slowly.

"The time for the Green Ninja to face his destiny has grown nearer," said Sensei Wu.

Lloyd looked at his friends. "I'm ready," he said confidently.

Lloyd's mind was racing. Now that he was older, he would be able to control his Spinjitzu better. But did he really have what it took to become the legendary Green Ninja?

Sensei Wu seemed to read his mind. "The time until the final battle has become shorter," he said. "But the Green Ninja has grown stronger!"